przypadkowy

# CONTINGENCY PLAN

emergency plan

## LOU ALLIN

RAVEN BOOKS
*an imprint of*
ORCA BOOK PUBLISHERS

**Library and Archives Canada Cataloguing in Publication**

Allin, Lou, 1945–
Contingency plan / Lou Allin.
(Rapid reads)

Issued also in electronic formats.
ISBN 978-1-4598-0114-1

1. Readers for new literates. I. Title. II. Series: Rapid reads
PS8551.L5564C65 2012      428.6'2      C2012-902563-1

First published in the United States, 2012
**Library of Congress Control Number:** 2012938192

**Summary:** Sandra Sinclair realizes she's made a terrible mistake in
marrying into an abusive relationship, putting herself and her
twelve-year-old daughter in grave danger. (RL 3.8)

*Orca Book Publishers is dedicated to preserving the environment and has
printed this book on paper certified by the Forest Stewardship Council®.*

Orca Book Publishers gratefully acknowledges the support for
its publishing programs provided by the following agencies:
the Government of Canada through the Canada Book Fund and the
Canada Council for the Arts, and the Province of British Columbia
through the BC Arts Council and the Book Publishing Tax Credit.

Design by Teresa Bubela
Cover photography by Getty Images

ORCA BOOK PUBLISHERS
PO Box 5626, Stn. B
Victoria, BC Canada
V8R 6S4

ORCA BOOK PUBLISHERS
PO Box 468
Custer, WA USA
98240-0468

www.orcabook.com
Printed and bound in Canada.

15  14  13  12  •  4  3  2  1

*With many thanks to Carolanne Papoutsis,*
*Vancouver Island's best eagle-eyed reader.*

# CHAPTER ONE

Nothing attracts attention like a dead whale.

A dozen people peered at a huge black carcass beached at low tide. Seagulls shrieked and dipped. Andy and I had loved picnicking at Aylard Farm Park. From here we would gaze across the glorious Strait of Juan de Fuca. Only two years ago. It seemed like ten.

Shortly after retiring early and moving to Vancouver Island, Andy was diagnosed with testicular cancer. Never a complainer, he'd been ignoring the symptoms. Half a year later he was ashes for our climbing red rose. The way he'd suffered, I was glad for his release. "Let go, love," I'd said, holding his hand on that last morning. "Jane and I will be fine." He squeezed back until my fingers ached. Then he was gone.

The mighty whale, collapsed under its own weight, lay on the exposed tidal shelf. People were circling, even touching it. One teen was using a sharp rock to cut off pieces of skin. What the hell was wrong with some people?

I headed back through the bushes to the main path. Why had I thought coming here would cheer me up? Tears blurred my vision. I shoved my chilly hands into my pockets. One foot caught on a gnarly root. I would have gone sprawling, but a hand grabbed my arm.

"Whoa! Watch that first step. It's a killer," a deep male voice said.

I'd ripped my tights, nothing worse. Still kneeling awkwardly in the weeds, I looked up at my Good Samaritan. The sun backlit his head like a halo. By his side was a border collie pup that began licking my face. It had a heart-shaped black mark on its white muzzle. *dog face*

"Scout, watch your manners. Not every lady likes doggy kisses. Up we go," he said, pulling me to my feet. I braced myself against a gigantic Sitka spruce. "Anything sprained? Can you stand?"

I cleared my throat, feeling like a fool. *stupid* Then I noticed a burning, prickly feeling on my hand. "Ouch," I said. I shook it to relieve the discomfort. "What did I land in?" A spindly plant surrounded me.

"Stinging nettle. Let's see," he said, taking my palm and examining it. "Wash it well with soap and water. It'll only bother you for a day or so. Not like poison ivy."

"Lucky me then," I said. I frowned. Acting crabby in front of a complete stranger.

"My name's Joe Gillette. There are some moist wipes in my car. I always plan ahead. Coffee too, if you take it black."

His brown eyes sparkled, honest as a calf's. A stranger looking at me like this was a new experience. I felt girlish and shy, despite my age. I'd been married for the last fifteen years. The last time I'd dated before that...one pathetic, forgettable evening with a friend's brother. All he could talk about was his mother's pot roast.

Five different answers raced through my mind. None of them sounded right. An eyebrow arched and Joe looked off at Scout chasing a seagull. "If you're okay, then..."

"Sorry," I said, blushing. "Coffee would be super." I almost added "kind sir." Soon I'd be curtsying. Wet wipes? Did he have a child? Was he divorced? Few people came here alone. The coastal trail was a place for serious hikers, while the park attracted families.

I followed him to his shiny black X-6 with a 1-LGL-EGL plate (one legal eagle?), parked near my rusty Neon. Given the soothing towelette, I wiped my hand. The prickly sensations eased.

"Feel better?" he asked. A corner of his expressive mouth rose.

I nodded and looked around. "There's a place we can sit."

At a nearby picnic table, we talked over the excellent Kona coffee he'd had shipped from Hawaii. Joe was a lawyer, he said, working with the elderly. "I'm no hot-shot criminal attorney like in the movies, but I feel good about what I do. Estate planning takes plenty of care. Elders are so vulnerable. Meet the King of Loopholes. Every penny counts for those folks. I can chase a deduction faster than a ferret after a mouse."

His friendliness was relaxing me. "Hey, liking your job is important. If you can help others, bonus."

"And yourself? Sounds like you care too. Social worker? Teacher? You can't be a nurse or doctor. They know about nettle."

It sounded more sincere than patronizing. I liked the fact that he was assuming I had a profession.

"I worked with my husband Andy. He… passed last year." I gave a few brief details. A story told too many times. Poor pathetic widow. Andy made me swear not to waste the rest of my life grieving.

"Sorry for your loss," Joe said, the lines around his mouth deepening in concern. A moment of silence followed. "Andy must have been a special man. What business were you in?"

"We owned a motorcycle and snow-mobile shop. Quads, too, and boats in the summer. Dawson Creek."

He gave a low whistle and a mock shiver. "I like to *go* to the snow. Not have it come to me. Some Canadian, eh? What's it like way up north, bush woman?"

That made me laugh. The unfamiliar sound amazed me. Who was that woman? "It's funny, but I miss the snow. It made everything clean and bright in the winter. Cross-country skiing, snowshoeing."

"Some people can't take the dreary rain from November to April, but remember that you—"

I finished his sentence. "—don't have to shovel it." That bond had us both grinning.

Scout bounded back with a stick and dropped it, his rear end up and wiggling in play mode. Joe tossed it again and again. Finally the dog flopped down, panting with his long, comical tongue. "Usually I get tired before he does."

At last I had to check the time. Swimming at the rec center ended in twenty minutes.

I hoped he didn't hear me sigh. "I'd better go. I have to pick up my daughter."

He smiled and cocked his head. "But you're so young. Day care?"

Even if he was teasing, I was flattered. I'm thirty-six, hardly a teenager. Somehow it coaxed a chuckle. My smiling muscles almost hurt from lack of use. "She's twelve. And look who's talking. You're the one with the towelettes," I said.

"*Semper paratus*. Always prepared with a contingency plan. I was an eagle scout. Won every medal. Even cooking. And by the way, you haven't told me your name," he added.

"It's S-s-sandra, Sandra Sinclair." I'd never stuttered before in my life.

"And your daughter?"

"Jane." I was glad there was no *S* in her name.

He nodded. "Sweet and old-fashioned. Good for you. My aunt's name was Jane.

There are way too many Brittanys and Brandys."

"And Lindseys and Nikkis," I added, joining in the entertainment-industry game. "Scarletts, Angelinas. I think we're dating ourselves." More confident by the minute, I gave him a more assessing look. A brush of gray at the temples of his chestnut-brown, razor-cut hair. Fresh-shaven face with a strong jawline. I pegged him in his early forties. Flirting was coming awfully easily.

"Dating *myself* was not what I had in mind," Joe said. "I wonder if I dare ask for your cell number. If you like to visit Aylard Farm, we have something in common already."

I felt my face blush when I answered. Should I have asked for his? Would he really call? And then what? This was happening all too fast, like a dam bursting. A quick check of his left hand showed no ring.

Even so, some married men didn't wear them. Or he could have removed it. Was I naïve or optimistic? My head was turning every which way *and* loose.

# CHAPTER TWO

A week later, cooking Jane's favorite chili, I was surprised to get a call. "Sandra? I hope you won't consider this too bold, but would you like another encounter with stinging nettle?"

"Joe, it's great to hear from you." I put down the spoon. "I've had enough acquaintance with that plant, thanks. Are you joking?"

"It will be far more pleasant. This time you will be in charge of the introductions. Trust me. I can pick you up about nine on Saturday. The city is so busy and noisy with tourists now that summer is nearly here. I usually drive into the country on weekends."

I hesitated. People might think a twelve-year-old daughter was old enough to be left alone, but I'd grown extra cautious since Andy died. My girl was precious. "I'm not sure I can find a sit—"

"Not to worry. Jane is invited. That's why I chose this place. Lots for kids to do."

A minute later he had my address, and I was marking my calendar for my first date since I was twenty-one.

* * *

That Saturday we took the Island Highway out of Victoria and up the scenic Malahat. We drove to a farm set up like a county fair. "This is the best time of year for stinging nettle," Joe said, keeping us guessing.

"I didn't know that," Jane said politely from the backseat. "I brought my plant guidebook. There are so many different plants down south." Natural sciences were her favorite subject. She had identified over one hundred plants for a school project. Back in Dawson Creek, the seven-month winter had left little time for botany.

We could hear her turning pages. Then she said, "Hey, young nettle is a double for spinach."

"You're on the right track, professor," Joe answered, flashing a wink at me.

After parking the car, Joe got tickets for our lunch. We toured the exhibits and bought jars of fireweed honey and lemon verbena jam. In a century-old apple orchard with picnic tables, our feast began. Green Goddess nettle soup followed by nettle salad with quinoa, chicken and nettle pesto with orzo. For dessert, a nettle cobbler. Who would have thought?

Kids were stuffed with veggie hotdogs, milk and brownies, which suited Jane. She used her best manners with *please* and *thank you*. I was so proud. She seemed to appreciate that Joe had made an effort to involve her.

An older teenager from the farm came over to the tables. He held a small gadget with a screen. "Hey, kids, let's go find some caches with the GPS."

"Cool," a youngster beside us said. Several others got up to follow, including Jane. I was pleased to see a rare smile on her face as she waved at me. Andy's little tomboy princess. Instead of a Barbie doll, he'd given her a Swiss Army knife and a small ax for Christmas when she turned nine. Then they went camping up near Watson Lake by the Yukon border. They built their own shelter, and he shot a couple of grouse to roast on the fire. Andy had a First Nations grandfather who taught him everything. Jane told me how Andy had skinned the birds by standing on the wings and pulling. Video games and designer clothes didn't interest her. That was fine with me. Girls needed to get close to nature, not study to be beauty queens.

I found myself telling Joe about growing up in Vancouver. My parents had died in a car crash ten years ago. My surviving grandmother was in a nursing home in Alberta. He told funny stories about law school and a hundred lawyers at the bottom of the sea being "a good start." The afternoon passed so quickly that I hardly realized when five o'clock rolled around.

Jane came back talking about "travel bugs" and trophy coins, interested in getting a GPS to hunt caches around Sooke. That was the first time she'd asked for anything other than a new bike. "We'll check online, honey," I said. Sounded expensive.

After fish and chips at Salty's in Mill Bay, Joe drove us back to our Sooke townhouse. There was my rattletrap Neon, pouting. I missed the comfort of our big commercial truck. We'd sold our GMC 3500 4x4 when we left the North.

In Joe's backseat, Jane's head was pillowed on the plush leather. She was fast asleep, seat belt and all.

"Thanks, Joe," I whispered before I woke her. "It's the first fun she's had in…far too long. She's only started to make friends here." Jane was a bit shy and studious. Life near a major urban area was more complicated than in small-town Dawson Creek.

"Losing a parent can be rough," Joe said, turning off the motor. "My dad died in a tractor accident when I was only eight. I have something in common with Jane."

"Sorry to hear that," I said. "And your mother?"

"She and my sister still live on our family farm in New Brunswick. They lease out the fields and run a B and B. I don't see them very often, I'm sorry to say."

"So your mom never remarried?"

He lifted a small, pearl-handled knife from the console. "Dad gave me this the year he died. He was only a farmer, but he was a prince to her. I guess she knew she'd never find another like him. Sometimes I wish she had. Not for my sake, but for hers."

I didn't want the evening to end. It was refreshing to talk to an adult. "Would you like a coffee? I can—"

Joe cocked a thumb toward the back. "We'd better get this little sleepyhead to bed. I have a really early day tomorrow too. And I'll be out of town in Toronto for a few weeks. But…" His smile lit up the night as he leaned forward. I could smell his citrus cologne. "I'll call you as soon as I get back."

"I'd like that." Something seemed different, I'd been thinking. Now I realized what was missing. "Hey, where's Scout?" I asked. Most outdoor venues on the island admitted dogs.

He firmed up his mouth and shook his head. "I took him to work when I could, even to the park twice a day. He didn't like staying alone at the condo. Howled until the neighbors complained. Guess it was stupid to think I could take care of such an active breed. The shelter told me he'll be easy to adopt. Border collies are popular. A nice family with two kids was already looking at him."

I was sorry about Scout. He was probably right. A family would appreciate a young dog. Our old shepherd Freya had gone to Rainbow Bridge the year Andy was diagnosed. Jane missed her.

There was a greenbelt around the townhouse with plenty of walking territory along the creek...maybe a dog might help Jane.

One step at a time, Sandra.

\* \* \*

Andy's Aunt Bonnie had been the main reason we'd moved to the island.

A retired bookkeeper, she lived in a cottage nearby on the Sooke Harbor. When we were there a few nights later for dinner, she noticed my happy mood. I told her about the date.

"About time, girl," Bonnie said with an understanding nod. "Nothing like a new man in your life to make those eyes sparkle."

"Come on, Bonnie. He's hardly *in* my life. One afternoon." In spite of my caution, happiness welled up inside me. It had been such a long time. I realized how self-pitying I had been in my rut.

"Andy's been gone a year. You know that you promised you'd jump back into life. You're moving slower than a banana slug," she said, peeling potatoes.

I looked out the window. Jane was playing on the flats with two boys from the T'Sou-ke reserve.

"How does Jane feel about him?"

I sipped the cider. Sweet and tart. Like Bonnie, the old doll. "She hasn't said anything pro or con. Is that a good sign?"

"I like the fact that he included her."

"He did make an effort." I snagged a carrot stick from the veggie tray and munched. "Think I should call him?"

"Chase after a man until he catches you. It's simple. I'm old fashioned enough to think that two parents are better than one."

I chuckled. "You would have been a super mother, even single."

She wagged a spoon at me, frowning. "I turned down three proposals, I'll have you know. I was very particular. There was my job. Pretty soon twenty years had…" Bonnie wrinkled her nose. "Oooh, what's going on?"

I smelled something burning. When she opened the oven door, smoke billowed out. "Dang. I was sure I set this at three twenty-five, not four twenty-five," she said.

"That happened to me once," I said, bringing her the oven mitts. "I think we can rescue the casserole. Scrape off some of the top and add more milk." Her King Ranch Chicken was a favorite.

She wiped a strand of hair from her brow. "I should use my bifocals, I guess. But Coke-bottle lenses. Yuck. They make me feel ancient."

The door opened, and Jane came in with a pail of shellfish. "Mom, did you know they used to dig clams here even hundreds of years ago? Can we eat them?"

Bonnie and I exchanged amused glances. Every day brought something new for our bright girl.

* * *

When he returned from Toronto, Joe had made a list of every glamor spot on the island. Tofino was at the top, a five-hour drive to the wild west coast. I left Jane with Bonnie.

They had rented a pile of *Harry Potter* DVDs for a marathon at home.

When I saw the inn, I couldn't imagine what the weekend had cost him, gourmet meals included. He had booked a two-bedroom suite overlooking the Pacific, and the breakers crashed just for us. There was something so comforting about being sheltered inside while a great tempest raged. Wood crackled in the fireplace. When he smiled at me, the chemistry took my breath away. But it was more than the sheer power of sexual attraction. We seemed to connect.

"It's more dramatic in the winter storm season," he said as we clinked champagne flutes. "But I special-ordered some white-caps for you. And those sea otters playing down in the cove this afternoon were on the payroll." We stood gazing out the wall of windows.

"Have you been here before?" I asked, the bubbles tickling my nose. Then I realized the implications. Had I spoiled the moment? I turned away and bit my lip.

"Yes." His voice took on a bittersweet tone. He drained the glass and set it down. "With my wife."

"Oh, you've…never mentioned her," I said. Like a blow to the chest, this information hit me hard. How simpleminded I had been.

He looked down. "Hurts too much, I guess. Even after five years. She died in childbirth. Maybe we waited too late. She was nearly forty. When you're starting a career…"

I blinked in the silence. Time to keep my mouth shut and listen. It took a special man to confess this vulnerability.

"And the boy didn't make it either. We'd named him Seth. After my dad." His eyes misted over, and I took his hand. It was smooth and warm.

He led me to the sofa, where we sat quietly. I understood what the words

23

*companionable silence* meant. It happened when two people had a perfect under-standing. There was no need to fill the air with chatter. But every word counted. I drank in what he told me about his search for a soul mate. Second best wasn't good enough. Andy and I had felt the same way.

"What do you think, Sandra? Is it too soon for you to consider a serious relation-ship?" he asked. His tender mouth nuzzled my ear, sending a tingle to forgotten places.

I nodded and reached over to seal the bargain with our lips. We wouldn't need that second bedroom tonight.

\* \* \*

Later, unable to sleep, I silently padded onto the cedar deck to look at the stars. There was the Great Bear, with the Big Dipper in her belly. The wind had died into a gentle kiss of salty air. "Andy, it's all going so fast. What should I do?" I whispered.

In silent answer, a comet streaked across the black velvet sky. Andy had loved Jack London's wilderness stories, especially *The Call of the Wild*. The young American author had packed a lot of living into his few years. What had he said? "I'd rather be ashes than dust...I would rather be a superb meteor, every atom of me in magnificent glow, than a sleepy and permanent planet."

It was time to live again.

# CHAPTER THREE

Two months later we were married. Aunt Bonnie was my maid of honor, sparkling in a bright blue dress.

We were at the townhouse preparing for the ceremony when Joe's ringtone sounded. "Home Sweet Home" by Mötley Crüe. What a sentimental guy.

He was grinning as he handed his cell to me. "Mom wants to talk to you. All the way from Quispamsis."

"Welcome to the family, dear," a mellow voice said in an East Coast accent, a lilt of Irish. Her name was Sheila. "Hope you like your in-laws a bit on the crazy side. We mean no harm. Sorry Diane and I can't be there, but I sent you something. I'm sure your wedding is going to be lovely. I know my son."

"How kind of you. I'm sure we'll meet soon," I said, glancing at Joe. He was giving an *okay* sign. I returned the phone.

"Yes, Mom. Not to worry. It got here safely. Perfect timing," Joe said. "I can't wait to see her face. In fact, I'm not going to wait any longer."

After we hung up, Joe pulled a ring from his pocket. "This belonged to my grandmother. Her name was Ruby. Like the main stone, with a circle of diamonds. Your other hand looked so lonely."

"It's beautiful," I said, holding it to the light. "They don't make rings like this anymore. I'll treasure it." The his-and-hers wedding rings had been understated and simple. I loved them. But this was a family heirloom.

Joe had already given Bonnie a stunning orchid corsage. Jane got a small package. "Open it," he said, watching her with pleasure. He was a man with a plan all right. He'd made all the arrangements. The honeymoon was still a secret. I was so happy, even a tent in a provincial park would have been a palace. As long as we were together.

Jane unwrapped a GPS from a leather carrying case. "Yes!" She punched the air in delight, then started exploring the features.

"Now you'll always know where you are. That's very important." Joe handed her another package.

"Cool! Travel bugs. Thanks, Uncle Joe," she said.

"What are they, honey?" I asked.

"When you put one in a cache, someone who finds it can take it all over the world. They get tracked by the number."

I planted a kiss on his fresh-shaven cheek. I loved how nice that felt. His skin was so smooth. Andy had had to shave twice a day or give me whisker burn.

We were married by a local minister in the colorful late-September gardens at the Sooke Harbor House. Hosts of chrysanthemums and dahlias surrounded us. A few tourists on their way to Whiffen Spit, below the inn, stopped and clapped for us when we kissed.

Our private dining room had a view of the bay, and the five-course meal featured smoked salmon soup and crab. Joe allowed Jane a sip of champagne.

"Mom, it's going to make me sneeze," Jane said, laughing.

"You'll get used to it, princess," Joe said. "All the men will be lining up for you in a few years."

"Here's an old Irish toast," Bonnie said, hoisting her glass. "May the sun…no, that's not right. May the road…I mean the wind…"

We made a joke about her being tipsy.

Joe rose to save the moment, ending with "May God hold you in the palm of his hand." Bonnie was forgetting more lately. Was it age or the beginnings of dementia? Andy hadn't mentioned that horror in his family, had he? I didn't want to think about that. Not today.

"I have another surprise, ladies," Joe said as we finished our Chocolate Decadence. He handed me a brochure from his inside pocket. "So I hope you're packed, all of you. We're leaving tomorrow afternoon for Disneyland. No excuses."

"Joe, you aren't serious. That's too gener...generous," I said. The wine and brandy were making everything a bit unreal. My tongue was stumbling over the longer words.

"It's time my girls got spoiled," he said, pulling out his phone. "I've been waiting a long, long time to be the man of the house. Now smile, all of you. Smile for my mom."

As he checked the pictures, I turned away to the view of the harbor. A bald eagle was soaring. Then another smaller bird. His mate? It felt warm and cozy being a family again.

* * *

The four days in California went so fast. Aunt Bonnie and Jane made the rounds of the rides, while Joe and I had time to ourselves. We drove along the scenic coastline in a splashy Mustang convertible, enjoying leisurely lunches. Each night at dinner we'd meet Jane and Bonnie back at the hotel.

"Thanks for your blessing, Andy," I said in my prayers as the plane headed back to our island. How many lucky women had had two wonderful men in their lives?

With the recession, we sold the small townhouse in Sooke below assessment value and put the money into long-term bonds as Joe suggested. What did ten or twenty thousand dollars more matter now? From the looks of Joe's condo in Victoria, he had been too modest about his finances. The Inner Harbor apartment was upscale with granite counters, a master suite bathroom and another for Jane. The view of Washington State and the white-capped mountains of the Olympic range took my breath away.

One day at our former place, I was raking the last leaves before the new people moved in. I thought I saw someone walking Scout by the mailboxes.

I walked over and knelt down to pet the dog. Same black mark on his muzzle, but he was growing into an adolescent. He kissed me over and over. "He likes you," the older woman said.

"Yes, I know Scout. My husband had to give him up. You must have been the people looking at him the day he came to the shelter."

She shook her head. "There must be some mistake. He was running loose down at French Beach. We called the CRD and no one had reported him missing. So he's found a home with us." French Beach was almost 20 kilometers west.

I didn't know what to say. Driving home half in a trance, I felt my stomach turning over. When I nearly hit a woman in a crosswalk, I pulled over and took deep breaths.

When I told Joe later, he said, "No way. I left him at the shelter in Saanich. That's sixty or more kilometers from French Beach."

"I guess so, but he looked so similar. And he was friendly."

"Honey, border collies are engineered to look similar. When I got him at the breeder, all his siblings had exactly the same markings. And what pup wouldn't love you?" He hugged me and planted a kiss on my ear. If you want, I can call the shelter and check."

"No, I'm sure you're right, Joe."

Jane was staying with Bonnie in Sooke during the week until the fall term ended. Joe had plans for her to start at St. Anne's, a private school in Victoria. "Our brilliant daughter will get the stimulation and opportunity she needs. I wouldn't be surprised if she went all the way to a PhD. First one in the family."

Jane had showed me the catalog that Saturday morning. Joe was right about the challenge. She'd been at the top of her class, bored most of the time. St. Anne's curriculum looked almost like a university's. "There's a special environmental studies program, Mom." I thought she was going to dance around the room.

Joe laughed as he poured a glass of champagne, something he vowed we'd have every night for our first month. "When the winter semester starts, we'll all be here. For only a while," he said. "It's too small, don't you agree?" Of three bedrooms,

one was his home office where he sometimes worked in the evening. He and two
other lawyers shared offices on Fort Street.

"You're probably right. Everything went
at warp speed after the wedding. Getting the
house ready to sell and then moving here."

He caressed my shoulder, finishing with
a gentle kiss on the cheek. "Sweetheart,
when I decide I want something, look out,
world. I've been keeping a secret from you
two. Time to fess up." He moved to an
elegant rolltop desk. Back he came with a
set of drafting plans.

"Joe, what in—?"

He touched a finger to my lips. "Uh-uh.
Look first. Talk later. We can change
anything you like, darling."

The blueprints and sketches showed
a spectacular West Coast–style home in
the nearby hills. "I've owned five prime
acres in the Highlands since I moved to
the island. The well's already in," he said.

"Take your time. This is the first house I've built too. I've been planning it in my head for years. Now what's on your wish list? You love cooking, so if you want an even bigger kitchen, or…"

"I never dreamed of a custom-built house," I said. My heart was singing. With our seasonal business, Andy and I had to watch our pennies.

"Plenty of privacy too," he added. "I've had enough of the noisy city." Even with triple-paned glass, you could hear the rush of the traffic. Victoria's zoning laws prevented extreme high-rises where the busy streets were far below.

In all the excitement, another thought hit me. "But out in the Highlands, what about my job? That's a long commute," I said.

I had been working part-time as a library assistant in Sooke. I liked helping people, but frankly, Jane and I had needed the cash. The cost of living on the island was nearly

double what we'd had to pay in the North.
Joe waved his hand. "No problem taking
off a few months, half a year, is there?
I'm going to need your expert opinion
on every inch of this home. Our home.
How does that sound, Mrs. Gillette?"
He held me at arm's length, pride glowing
in his eyes.

I nodded as he turned back to the blueprints. He'd done so much work. If I really
missed the job once the house was finished,
I could try my luck at one of the closer
regional library branches. On second thought,
a volunteer job would be easier to get and
more flexible. A guide at Craigdarroch Castle
or another tourist attraction might be interesting. Or charity work. That might be good
for a lawyer's business.

* * *

In January, Jane was enrolled at St. Anne's.
She loved the challenging courses. She'd even

joined the lacrosse team. Family dinners were full of laughter.

I spent my days touring furniture stores, choosing flooring, cabinets, countertops, lighting. Joe had been right. It was a full-time job. No sooner did one stage finish, than the next began. I was pressed to get home by five thirty, which left little time to prepare dinner.

One day I wasn't back until six. I bustled through the door and took the groceries to the kitchen. Five squares of linoleum fell to the floor. Joe came in from the living room, a scotch in his hand. "Sandra, you should have called. What's going on?" He looked more annoyed than worried.

"The flooring guy wasn't back from a job. Samples were missing. I had to wait half an hour. Then there was a jam on Douglas. Traffic was re-routed." Why was I having to explain myself?

"Huh. I have a good mind to take our business elsewhere." He finished his glass.

"Call that catering place over on Gorge. Order whatever's fastest. And next time check in. That's what a cell's for."

As I picked up the phone, I saw five more decorating magazines that Joe had brought home. There was my reading for tonight. I could put my novel away.

* * *

Five months later we moved into our dream home. Eight thousand square feet of cedar, glass, steel and concrete. A lap pool. Solarium. State-of-the-art video room with leather recliners. Steam washer and dryer. Exercise room with treadmill, elliptical trainer and Bowflex.

One night I was on my laptop at the kitchen table, toying with window-dressing ideas for the downstairs suite. Swatches were spread out around me. Joe had said he wanted his mother and sister to have their own area when they visited. Funny that they hadn't called since our wedding day or after I sent a handwritten thank-you note for the ring. We'd all been so busy. I hoped that they were all right.

"Why not have your mom and sister come visit now? The guest suite upstairs is perfect for them," I said to Joe.

He was laughing at several humming-birds dueling at the feeder. Seconds went by before he answered. "There's the B and B. They have chickens, and a few goats and horses. Mom still wants to be a farm woman in those small ways. It takes work to arrange for someone to care for the animals. Anyway, we're not a super clingy family. Just there for each other. That's what counts."

"I guess so." Possibly we could fly to the East Coast at Christmas.

A short while later, Jane came running toward me in tears. "It's gone, Mom."

I stood up. "What's gone?"

"My final science project. It's due tomorrow. Intertidal species, remember? There's a big blue screen with warning messages. Everything's, like, frozen." Her small fists were clenched. She looked so vulnerable and defeated even though she was nearly as tall as I was.

We hurried to her room, and I took a look. Joe was passing by in a fluffy white robe, his hair wet from a shower. "Did I hear female distress calls? What's up, ladies?"

Jane stuttered out computer language I didn't understand.

He sat at the screen and fiddled. "Do you have a memory stick, Jane?" he asked. She got him one.

Jane was struggling not to cry.

"No luck retrieving the data," he said after a minute. He stood. "It must have been that power surge this morning."

The lights had gone off when a transformer blew down the road. We'd seen the BC Hydro truck and its cherry picker.

"But ours are okay," I said in confusion. "You were on earlier. I'm on the Internet. Why Jane's?"

He shrugged. "The way things are routed, the data comes into her computer first. Jane's took the hit." He gave her a cool and assessing look. "Didn't you have a contingency plan?"

She gulped, wiping her eyes. "What's a contin—?"

"It means a backup plan. Automatic data retrieval. For the entire hard drive. Not just your current projects."

"But I never thought...I mean, I have a surge protector." Jane bent under the desk and pointed to the unit.

Joe took one look. "These cheap ones you brought from your old place are no better than a multiple outlet. This will be a lesson for you, Jane. A valuable one. Learn from it."

He left us alone, whistling a tune as his footsteps faded down the hall. I hardly knew how to react. This was a new side. Not that he'd been abusive or raised his voice, but his reaction seemed very cold. Jane looked like a wounded puppy. Not only did she blame herself, but I could see that she was disappointed in Joe.

"Chin up, my girl. I'll get a coffee, you get a pop, and we'll use my computer and whatever data you still have. If I know you, it's still fresh in your mind."

Jane had too much pride to let the project go. Together we worked all night reassembling the material. She had the resource books and knew the websites.

When Jane brought home a C plus instead of her usual A, I thought again about the way Joe had acted that night. Maybe he'd been tired. Maybe he was trying to make Jane more independent. I had never thought about the backup. I assumed kids knew more about computers.

Maybe that was the point though.

She was a kid.

# CHAPTER FOUR

O ver his favorite buckwheat-pancake breakfast, I told Joe that I was going to start looking for another job. "The house is, for all purposes, finished."

A glint of frost passed across his handsome features. He folded his serviette in six. "The house, maybe, but what about the landscaping? Don't quit on me now, Sandra. I need your input. The jewel needs a proper setting," he said. He gestured toward the window, at the expansive yard that tumbled away from the house. "Don't you want fruit trees, rhodos, perennial beds, the rock garden, the koi pond?"

All of those ideas had been his dreams. I wasn't much for gardening. Now I felt selfish. "I know we talked about it, Joe."

"Don't you want our place to be perfect? Where are your priorities? Is it a question of money?"

"You've been very generous." *First class all the way* was his motto.

He came around the table and put an arm around me, drawing me close. "Don't I work long hours to earn enough to surround you and Jane with the best? Sure, it's an adjustment from your other…life, but is it that hard?"

I blinked. That stung. "Of course it's not." A month or two. How long could it take? I swallowed my disappointment. I felt like a prisoner. Maybe working in the yard would help.

"That's more like it," he said as he got up to go to work. "Start calling and make a list of contacts for these jobs by the end of this week. We can look it over together on the weekend. Hire women when you can. They don't show up hungover or steal tools like men do."

* * *

The next day my Neon died. At the garage, they told me that the repairs would exceed the car's value. I called a dealer and was given a reasonable quote for the same basic transportation. What more did I need?

I waited until we were having our after-dinner coffee and Jane was in her room, downloading music.

"Another shitbox ready to collapse in an accident?" Joe asked after I'd explained my day. "You're much more valuable to me than that, darling girl. Besides, I don't want you driving all over when you should be home thinking about dinner. Thinking about making every meal even better than the last."

A burning sensation seeped into my chest. Joe was always demanding more, setting up another hoop to jump through. My jaw clenched and I looked away.

He sighed. "If you must have one, wait until I make a couple of calls about when the new models come in. A guy at BMW owes me big-time. Once you drive a Bimmer, you won't want anything else."

Getting around until then wouldn't be easy. We lived far from a bus route. And I couldn't bring myself to spend the seventy dollars for a round-trip in a taxi.

As I was loading the dishwasher, another landscaper called back. After setting up an appointment, I went outside to look around and organize my thoughts. The house did look like a castle. Maybe more greenery would soften the severe effect. Virginia creeper turned so pretty and red in the fall. I'd never dreamed of living like this. But instead of being proud, I was getting anxious. Why couldn't I make Joe happy? He'd given us everything.

\* \* \*

When the summer holidays arrived, Bonnie was having a problem with driving and stopped coming over. "I'm worried about her, Joe," I said during a commercial break in the news. "She says her vision is bothering her, but it's more than that."

"She's a busybody, Sandra. When you're with her, you're living in the past. With Andy. The old bat fills your head with silly ideas when you should be thinking about how to make this marriage work better."

I felt a chill. His words about her sounded cruel. "Work better. What do you mean?"

He straightened his shoulders as he poured a second brandy and turned off the TV. "Don't delude yourself into thinking that I haven't noticed the change in your lovemaking. You're so remote. Like it's a chore. What's wrong? Now that you've gotten what you wanted, you take me for granted."

His comment rocked me. The dissatisfaction was moving to another level. "You're wrong. I haven't—"

With two quick steps, Joe moved in front of me. Veins stood out on his temple and his hot breath made me flinch. I leaned backward.

"What did you say? Did I hear you right?"

"I said you were...wrong. Please don't talk so loudly. What if Jane comes—?"

"I'll do what I please in the house I bought...for *us*, woman. And I'll tell you something else. I am *never* wrong."

He stormed out, slamming the door. His suv screamed up the drive, scattering gravel. Suddenly I felt very alone. To distract myself, I emptied the dishwasher. Then I watered the houseplants. I looked out the front window. No sign of his car. I ground fresh beans and filled the coffeemaker. Would he be back by breakfast?

When Jane walked in later, I was reading in bed. Or trying to. I couldn't concentrate. My eyes were hot and stinging from tears of frustration and worry. I could hardly swallow.

"It turned out perfect. Not one burnt kernel," she said, offering me some popcorn.

"No thanks, sweetie," I said. One hand was shaking, and I covered it with the book.

She looked at me oddly. "Sure. Where's Uncle Joe, anyway?" He hadn't asked her to call him *Dad*. That was fine. *Uncle* was still respectful.

"He...had some business."

"You okay?" she asked.

I missed the times together with just the two of us. We made a good team. "A silly argument. You know grown-ups."

She sat down on the bed next to me. Outside an owl hooted. "He's not the same, is he? He used to be so nice. Maybe *too* nice. Do you think he was pretending? Until you got married?"

"Don't be silly, honey."

*Too nice. Pretending.* Kids came to the point in so few words.

Was she right?

* * *

Around four in the morning I finally fell asleep. I wished that I had something warm to hold. Even a cat. But Joe said litter boxes "polluted" the house.

At daybreak, I didn't want to open my sore eyes. Then I smelled something floral. A dozen red roses lay on the pillow beside me. Warm muffins, whipped butter and orange juice were carefully arranged on a bed table, the linen clean and crisp.

"Sorry, my angel. I've been overdoing it lately. Nothing serious. Just not up to snuff. I was so wrong to take it out on you.

Can you find it in your generous heart to forgive me?" he asked.

Visions of Andy returned. He'd been grouchy in the months before his diagnosis. His burden, trying to protect us while hoping that his illness would resolve itself.

"Joe, you're all right, aren't you? You're not—"

"A few problems at work. Comes with the territory. I let them get to me." He stroked my arm with gentle fingers. "Let's get our groove back. It can't have gone far."

I took a sip of juice. Fresh-squeezed. And where had he gotten the roses at this hour?

We talked it out. Things would get better. There wasn't that much more to do on the landscaping. The cedar hedge. A twig arbor I'd seen on a gardening show. Then in the fall, outside chores would soon end. He had a lot on his mind in that high-powered job. Success came at such a terrible price.

# CHAPTER FIVE

One afternoon a week later, I went into Joe's office to look for a stapler. I couldn't see it on the desk and opened a drawer. He walked through the door.

"What the hell do you think you're doing?" After slamming the door, he marched over. His rigid and powerful posture dared me to speak.

"Nothing, I only wanted…a s-stap—" I fumbled my words.

"Do I mess with your stuff?" he demanded.

I stared.

"Well, do I? Have I ever rummaged through your desk?" His face was scarlet, and a pulse drummed in his temple. His fists opened and closed as if they had a mind of their own.

What could I say?

"No, but—"

"Then stay away from mine." His brows were stormy. "I hate it when things are out of order. What if I couldn't find something? I'm a lawyer. Time is money. And I don't want to have to tell you this again. Have some respect."

"Yes, Joe."

"What's the matter with you anyway? Is there someone else? Is that why you're always on that bloody computer? Your stuttering is a dead giveaway that you're guilty about something." He stepped back and folded his arms, assessing me.

Undressing me. Stripping me to the core.

"What? That's ridiculous." The idea was so preposterous that I let out a laugh.

"You have some nerve telling ME not to be silly, missy. Do you live in some kind of dream world? You've never had a real job in your life, have you?"

"You know I worked with Andy." I kept my voice low and reasonable. What if I stuttered again?

"Big deal." He waved his hand in dismissal. "At some mom-and-pop business, barely hanging on. Why are you always talking about him? Andy is dead. I'm not. Stop rubbing my face in it. Do you know how you sound?" he demanded, his eyes blazing with contempt. "*Do* you?"

* * *

After the stapler issue, the more I tried, the more he criticized. If I did one thing, I should have done another. One rule, two, then more and more. He kept me off balance. I wondered if he could follow my trails on the computer. Just in case, I erased everything.

One afternoon I was on a chat line with other women. They were talking about methods their abusive spouses used to control them. Just like Joe did. The word *sociopath* emerged. Until then, I had thought it applied only to criminals. Killers. But that wasn't true. Sociopaths could be leaders. Many ran successful businesses. They could be charming. When it suited them. They said whatever worked. They felt nothing. Ordinary rules didn't apply to them.

I needed to learn more. This was new, but it explained so much. I didn't dare put a password on my computer. Like before, he'd find a reason to use it. Then he'd get really mad. The walls were closing in.

We hadn't had sex for weeks. His punishment? I didn't care.

Jane returned from a school geocaching club trip to Washington State. I was glad she had gone. Our fights couldn't be hidden anymore.

"He's worse, isn't he, Mom?" she had said.

"I don't know, baby." But I did. "I guess I…"

"Mom! It's not *you*. Why can't you see that?"

"He has changed. But maybe it's stress at work. That affects people in different ways. Just give it a little more time."

"I don't understand why you keep…" Her voice trailed off as she turned away in disappointment.

He began ignoring both of us. That was almost worse than abuse. Like we didn't exist. For once I stopped crawling to get back into his graces. He ate out and came home late to his own ensuite bedroom. The tension in the house made it hard to breathe. I started thinking about the heartbreaking version of his life that he had given me. What *had* happened to his wife? Had he even been married? Was he still married? Then who were these relatives?

"Mom," Jane said one night while we were doing dishes together. "I found out something. I didn't want to tell you until I was sure."

"What, hon? Another project?" I tried to smile at her, but I knew my face looked gray and drawn. No amount of makeup could mask the misery I felt.

"It's about Joe's mom and sister. In that little town in New Brunswick. The one with the funny name."

"What about them?" He never mentioned them on his own. When I asked, he repeated the same facts. Now and then he'd add another detail. Like he was making it up as he went along. Telling me what I wanted to hear.

"I made a Facebook friend there. In Quispamsis. She knows everybody. Her people have lived in the area for a hundred years. There's no Gillette family."

I turned off the water at the sink and looked at her. "What? And the B and B?"

She shook her head. "No one by that name with a B and B or a farm or anything. Honest. It's a small place. Like Dawson Creek."

What could I say?

I felt a core of steel streak down my backbone. Enough was enough.

* * *

The next morning Joe looked at me over the *Times Colonist*. His eyes had once seemed warm and brown. Now when I searched them, I saw through to nothing. Was he even human? What was happening to me? I thought about Bonnie and the way she imagined things. She'd called twice last week about a prowler. Her neighbor had suggested that she install motion-sensor lights. A midnight deer in search of roses was the culprit.

"Do you have something to tell me?" Joe asked. "I always know by that smirk on your face. You're such a child."

I flinched. This sounded like trouble. "What do you mean?"

"Don't play games, Sandra." He gripped my arm across the table. My coffee spilled onto the cherry wood. Joe liked it polished with lemon wax.

"Look what you've done. Stupid and clumsy." He released my arm as if I were a leper.

I wiped up the spill with my napkin.

"Don't use the linen serviette, you fool," he growled. "You don't deserve good things if you can't take proper care of them."

"Sorry." For the first time, I left it at that.

"Sorry. Sorry. Another day, another sorry." His eyes narrowed into laser beams. "And further…"

This was bad. "And further" meant that much more was coming. He shoved me backward in my chair. I was glad that Jane had gone to school.

"What the hell are you doing gossiping on the computer with those bitches? Nothing better to do?"

My heart beat in an overlap. In a few seconds, I might faint. "You mean—" I had the paralyzing feeling that I'd forgotten to clear everything. Bonnie had called in the middle of my session.

"That's right. I saw it on your computer." He glared at me. "Don't lie to me.

62

My keyboard's batteries died. We were out. I used yours to look up a stock quote. Guess what the history said."

"The history. You had no right." Another person seemed to say those words. I couldn't take them back.

"I have every right to know what my goddamn wife is up to. I never thought you'd be such a sneak. Why do you need strangers like that? Choosing them over me. Going around behind my back, making a mockery of my trust."

"Andy and I used each other's computers, but we always respected each other's privacy online. That's real trust." Deep in an untapped well, I found the strength to go even further. I stood and took a step toward him. "Speaking of honesty, why do you never hear anything from your mother? You told me she lived in Quispamsis. There's no one with that name there."

"What? Are you calling me a liar?" He gave me a shake that rattled my teeth.

But he didn't slap me.

My face would be unmarked. He was no fool.

No turning back. "I'm going to leave you, Joe." The statement seemed to come from someone else, a stranger who had had enough.

His eyes hardened into black diamonds. His low, deliberate voice chilled me. "That's the *one* thing you won't do, Sandra. Nobody leaves me. Nobody. You are an expensive investment in money and time."

"I will, and then I'll get a…a…restraining order." There it was. As a lawyer, he knew the process. My head was light. I filled my lungs with air and stood even straighter.

Standing up with his hands waving in a spooky mock-fear gesture, he laughed long and hard. "Don't believe what you see on television, Sandra. There's no protection for a greedy user like you. I get what I want when I want it. I have influential friends everywhere. At all levels. Don't be naïve."

This cruelty that I was seeing in Joe made me think back to Scout...What *had* happened to the dog? Why hadn't I read that first sign? It had seemed so insignificant at the time.

Was everything a lie?

\* \* \*

Joe was never gone overnight. The rare time he went to Vancouver for the day, I couldn't use his suv because he marked the mileage. He'd never again mentioned the new car he was going to get for me. My helplessness was part of his plan. Perhaps he thought I would beg him.

One day I called a number in the phone book. Del Finch, private investigator. "Find out what you can about Joe Gillette.

Don't contact me yourself. Wait for *my* call." A few hundred dollars from the household money would be the retainer.

"Missus, say no more. I'm used to these rules. And from what I'm hearing, you take care. And erase this call. Little mistakes can cost."

A week later I called him back. I'd had Jane buy a cheap cell phone at the drugstore. It was hidden in the potting shed, protected from the moisture in a ziplock baggie. Limited minutes on the card, but Jane could buy more when she went to school. We had become a team again for the worst reasons.

Finch cleared his throat before he began his report. "There have been some questions raised about his appropriating funds from elderly people. Getting them to name him in their wills. He's skated clear so far, but…"

"I'm not surprised." A man like that wouldn't have a clean, honest corner in his life.

"There's something else. His wife Chrissie died in a spring cross-country skiing accident several years ago in Alberta. They got off the main trails. She died of exposure. He barely made it himself. Three days went by before they were reported missing by concerned friends."

"Skiing? I thought she died in childbirth. He told me the name they'd picked for the—"

"Bullshit. There was no child. She had an insurance policy for a million dollars. Nice chunk of change. According to her family, she was very cautious. She never would have left the marked trail. Joe sued the lodge, but it was tossed out of court. The facts didn't make sense. They'd checked out, then left their car in a far lot and started into the backcountry. They obviously ignored the warning signs about keeping on the trails. And if they were lost, they did all the wrong things. Instead of staying put and making the universal distress signals, they'd kept moving. Search and Rescue was sent out, of course. Even helicopters. The tree cover was too thick. It was two more days before they found him."

I sat on a pile of bags of soil in the shed. The smell of moist earth surrounded me. I was potting paper narcissus bulbs for a fall forcing. Something to cheer up the house.

Now instead of life, I thought of death.

"Five days?" That sounds awfully risky." I said. "How was he saved?"

"Good question. But in spring, temperatures aren't that cold. My thought is that he kept his emergency supplies on him or had stashed them. Power bars maybe. Small heat packs. And of course he was much bigger. More fat and muscle. She wasn't more than a hundred and ten pounds. It was damned smart, if that's the right word. Took plenty of planning.

Nobody could prove a thing. And they never will."

I shuddered in spite of myself. What did he have in mind for me? A sailboat trip with a storm on the horizon? Both of us had taken out expensive policies with the idea that we were a family now.

It was more than money for him.

It was the arrogance of power.

# CHAPTER SIX

"Bye, Mom. I'm going to Mandy's. We're planting a geocache at the old bridge. Then we're making pizza."

"Have fun. Be back by nine. School tomorrow."

I watched my little girl as she bounced down the front walk toward the Sheftels' minivan. How had she grown so tall so quickly?

That night I made a gourmet meal that even Joe couldn't criticize. Shrimp cocktail, prime Alberta beef filets, creamed potatoes, Caesar salad, an Australian Shiraz that had cost fifty dollars, and chocolate cheese-cake for dessert. Joe never questioned bills for our home, clothes and dining.

"Now that's more like it, little one," Joe said, his face relaxed and approving for a change as he cleaned his plate. He flashed an *okay* sign. "You got the steaks just right. Perfecto."

I had also polished the silver and got the windows gleaming. How fake was my smile? What would he pick on next? What new rule would I break? It had taken a week of groveling to get back to this hell. But I had a good reason. Now I was ready to make plans.

"Cat got your tongue?" Joe asked after dinner. He played with a strand of my long blond hair as we sat on the sofa in front of the early news. I wondered if he was going to wind it around my neck.

We sat under the oil painting of me, based on a photo, that he'd commissioned.

It greeted me from above the marble fireplace the day we moved into the house. "My last duchess, like the poem by Browning," he had said. At first I thought the idea was charming.

Later, I'd found the lines in a book of verse. I wasn't so stupid about literature that I couldn't see the comparison. Another jealous husband. A young wife. End of story. As the Duke said, "I gave commands; then all smiles stopped…"

"Happy?" he asked as we finished our decaf. The cruel curve of his mouth froze me. The dimple on one cheek mocked all innocence. He was holding my hand so tightly that it ached.

"Who wouldn't be?" That pleased him. I prayed that he couldn't feel my heart breaking out of my chest.

"I keep my promises, darling. For as long as we both shall live. Remember that. You have a forever home. Good girls always do." He gave my ear a playful pinch.

"And Jane?"

"Bright little Jane will be off to university in a few years. I think back east. They have a world-famous marine biology program at Queen's. Then we'll have more time for ourselves. Won't that be wonderful?"

That night our lovemaking earned a solid-gold Oscar for me. For him, the usual silver star for excellence. My body responded in spite of itself. I was almost grateful. That helped the performance.

*   *   *

I started trembling as we lay like spoons, his favorite position. His arm pulled me closer. He read my fear as passion and began again. He'd had a shower earlier, but I could still smell his expensive cologne. Now it made me sick. Never was I so happy that he had agreed I should be on the pill. Bringing this man's child into the world would have been a death sentence.

At least Scout was safe. Joe's first wife Chrissie was beyond help. Jane and I had to find a place where he would never follow us.

I lay awake thinking. The property was in both our names. Everything else— at least everything I knew about—was held in joint accounts. I wouldn't have put it past him to be monitoring them to trap me.

Joe had turned away and was snoring. Moving like a zombie, I got up and went to the toilet. For several minutes, I retched silently with a towel over my mouth. Tears poured down my cheeks. His lovemaking felt like the coils of a serpent. Squeezing, squeezing. I was waiting for the perfect moment, but where could I get the money to leave?

Then I remembered.

The next morning, I talked with Jane. "Get those twenty-dollar American double-eagle coins Grandma left you." I had never mentioned them to Joe. They were my daughter's university fund. For years I had been watching their value rise as precious metals soared toward two thousand dollars an ounce. I'd never get full value, but I'd get enough.

Del Finch, the investigator, sold them for me in Seattle and kept a small percentage. He brought me forty thousand in large bills. We never met at the house. A woodland path behind our property led to a small stream where I walked and he waited.

I put my escape money in a box of sanitary pads for heavy periods. Heavy periods. Too right.

I worried about Bonnie. The weak link.

"I'm going to be…away for a while. Joe and I haven't been getting along," I said on the phone.

"Now, now, dear. Couples have silly fights all the time. It's natural. You both have to give more than fifty percent in a marriage. I suppose that's what they call a compro…

oh, something." She paused for so long that I thought we had been disconnected. "Is that the right word? I'm getting rather forgetful."

I told her that if she didn't hear from me for a few weeks that she wasn't to worry. "Our plans aren't fixed yet. Jane and I are going to get away from the city."

"But what about school, dear?"

"I've told the principal that it's a family emergency. Jane's bringing her books and assignments with her. St. Anne's is very flexible."

I would contact her when I found a safe way.

She gave a worried laugh. "You're acting so dramatic. Have you tried a marriage counselor? People should be able to work things out. Where will you ever find such a wonderful man like Andy? I mean…oh, dear."

"I love you, Bonnie. Take care." I swallowed back tears as I said goodbye. I hoped she didn't hear my voice breaking. It made me feel better that Sharon, her neighbor and friend of thirty years, was a nurse who looked in on her every day. She had experience in assisted living. Bonnie had also given her power of attorney years ago. At the time, Andy and I had lived too far away to be of regular help. Whether or not the women were more than friends, I didn't know. Love had many faces.

Joe's wasn't one.

* * *

Jane and I were playing Scrabble that night when I told her the plans. Joe had gone for a jog.

"He's evil, Mom. I know. I saw those bruises on your shoulders."

I had tried to keep the worst from her. Maybe that had been a mistake.

A question hung over my bowed head. What had I done to my daughter?

"He's never...touched you, has he?"
Would she have told me?

"No way!" Jane stood up and pushed
her tiles aside. "Why can't we tell the
police? Aren't they there to help us? I don't
understand."

"That's the problem, honey. He's never
going to leave us alone. It's not in his
nature. He didn't show me his dark side
until it was too late. Some people are so
dangerous that even the police can't help.
I'm sorry that I got us into this. But I'm
going to get us out. Here's what I've done
so far. You can be a big help."

The new identities cost ten thousand
dollars. Del had friends in the Vancouver
black market. When it was more conve-
nient, Jane did some transfers by meeting
Del at her school. The driver's license and
birth certificates were enough. Passports I
could never have afforded. Living outside
the country was beyond our reach.

But I was comfortable in the wilderness. That was a strength. And the hours were counting down. Freedom was calling my name.

Andy's grandfather had built a little trapper's camp in north central BC on Holy Cross Lake. Nothing fancy. Not even electricity when I'd been there. A retired logger, Tom Sinclair had belonged to the Cheslatta band, otherwise known as Carrier People or Dakelh. When a Dakelh man died, his widow carried around his bones and ashes for a period of mourning.

I'd been to the cabin once, on my honeymoon. And that's where I was headed now, my kid in tow.

Back to where Andy's family had been. It seemed like the one safe place.

The plan was to make our way off the island in an indirect way. The first places Joe would look would be the airlines. His money and power would buy any information he wanted. Being off the grid would help me. And I'd never mentioned the cabin. I was sure of that.

When I told Jane the plan, she looked almost relieved. "Good job, Mom," she said. "When do we go?"

"That's my girl," I said, pulling her close. She hadn't seen half what I had. He managed to hold himself in check in front of her. He didn't want any witnesses.

"It's not as different as last time when we moved," she said, sounding older than her years. "This is almost like going back to Dawson Creek."

"I'm proud of you, Jane. It's not easy to leave friends behind. If things work out, we can move to a larger city later. But we can't take any chances." Joe would never give up searching for us. Nobody took anything from him. The strong crushed the weak. They did what they did because they *could*.

* * *

Then to close an important deal, Joe had to go to Calgary for three days.

"I don't like leaving you two alone. Keep your cell handy. I'll be calling," he'd said, giving me a stern look. Jane and I saw him off at the airport. We even waved. That beautiful silver plane rose into the air, our hopes with it.

At the house, we took only our suitcases. Two lives in little parcels. Most of the expensive presents Joe had given me were vested in the house. A three-thousand-dollar espresso machine. A grand piano. The wine cellar. I planned to pawn the rings. The rubies and diamonds were real, Del's jewelry contact had said. We took a few clothes and pictures of Andy. His memory rode lightly in our hearts.

Under my new name, I had used a thousand dollars to buy a reliable old Bronco. I had left it in a mall parking lot. I asked our taxi driver to drop us off a few blocks away from downtown. At a pawnshop we got five thousand for the rings. I was taking no chances that Joe could trace the cab records and discover the Bronco.

Cash in hand, we hit the highway. We headed up island to Comox. From there we took a ferry to remote Powell River on the mainland. More direct routes to Vancouver seemed risky. Call me paranoid, but I was taking no chances. Still, I found myself looking over my shoulder. Every move was critical in this chess game. There were no do-overs.

At a cheap motel, I cut Jane's hair, bleached it, and set out the clothes we'd bought at Value Village.

"Mom, that's a pair of farmer's overalls. And that plaid shirt. How can I wear that?"

"Pretend we're in a play for the first few days. Let's make it a game. See if you can act like a boy."

She giggled, which relaxed the tension, and modeled in front of the cracked mirror.

"You mean, like, spit and swear? I'm allowed?"

With spray-gray hair and a frumpy dress, I was her grandmother. Dredging up some high-school French added to the illusion. Our paperwork read Suzanne and Denise Dupuis. Del had told me that most likely they were dead. Their names would have been taken from burial records back east. Only the ages would match. This unfortunate mother and daughter had given us a second life. I would remember them in my prayers.

We went to bed that night with the sound of trucks roaring by. Air brakes made the windows shake. The sheets were threadbare. Jane's pillow was ripped. Tiles were missing in the bathroom. Even the pizza we had ordered was cold. Through thin walls we could hear a drunken party with laughter and loud music.

I felt like I had gone to sleep in paradise.

# CHAPTER SEVEN

The coastal highway wound its way to the seaside town of Gibsons. We ate a burger and fries at a stand while we waited for the ferry across to Route 99 to Vancouver and then on to Route 1 east. Jane went for a walk. I admired the postcard glory of Howe Sound. Dark blue waters, light blue sky, white-capped mountains to the north where we were eventually headed. The green islands to the west looked so vulnerable. I'd have to forget the tang of salt air and the moan of foghorns. What did that matter if you lived in a prison with torture as your daily bread?

Jane came back with a whoop and showed me the GPS screen with a little treasure chest image. "I found a neat cache, Mom. It's called 'Rock-a-Bye, Baby,' and guess what? It was in a fake rock. Pretty cool, eh? Some guy who was caching told me there's a lot more..."

I nodded, only half listening.

Then I remembered something that froze me. Everyone knew cell-phone transmission could be located. One tower, another, then a third. Zeroing in by triangulation. That's why we weren't carrying a phone. What had Joe said to Jane when he gave her the GPS? *Now you'll always know where you are.* So could he find us if the unit was on? Even if it wasn't? If it had been rigged with a homing device? Joe could afford the best. Would he know that we'd left even if he were in Calgary?

"Turn it off," I said. "Please give it to me. No arguments."

Jane looked mildly hurt but obeyed. She followed as I went out of sight around a corner into a group of cedars. I smashed the screen with a large rock, then threw the unit 15 meters out into deep water.

"Mom! What—?" Tears welled in Jane's eyes.

"He may be using it to track us. I'm no expert, but we can't take the risk," I said. "Please try to understand, honey. I'm sorry I didn't think about it sooner."

"Can I get another one in Vancouver?"

"Sweetie, we can't stop right now. Later maybe."

Twenty minutes later we drove onto the ferry to North Van, the ramp clanking under us. The steel doors closed as a seagull flew out to freedom. Somehow I expected to see Joe's car behind us. Had I dodged a bullet? None too soon.

It took us two days to make our way to Williams Lake, careful to stay beneath the radar. We stayed in cheap roadside motels, empty of people now that October had arrived. If I saw one more greasy hamburger, I was going to scream. At least now we could take off our disguises.

Then came Quesnel and Prince George. The strong arms of the North folded around me. The sweet, clean air gave me hope. Grandpa Tom's camp was south of Vanderhoof. Tourism, logging and milling were the mainstays.

We picked up supplies in Fort Fraser, a town of only a hundred. Then we headed for Holy Cross Lake. The name felt blessed and safe.

Carrying the cash made me nervous, but the nearest bank was probably 80 kilometers away. The money would last us for a few years. What would happen when we ran out? Maybe I could pick up a job in the summer when tourists arrived.

Cleaning, cooking, money under the table. I couldn't think that far ahead.

Running for our lives made me feel like an animal. Always keeping my head down. Wondering where the next meal was coming from. Where we could sleep without one eye open. Could a deer escape a mountain lion? Gramps had said that all beasts had their special powers, even rabbits and deer. Rabbits were survivors through seasonal coloring. More than one man had been killed by a deer's hooves striking his chest. As for Joe? I saw him like a mountain lion.

Strong. Relentless.

Merciless.

I hadn't been to the old place in nearly fifteen years. Gramps didn't own the land. It was leased on a long-term basis. Suppose it were occupied, or worse, no longer standing?

I shook off my fears. People didn't care to live full-time in a rustic cabin. As for sturdiness, the camp was built to last.

*Please be here for us*, I prayed.

The four-wheel-drive Bronco turned out to be a good choice. We pulled onto a bush road, the snow-brushed ruts packed from the cold. When we neared the lake, the road forked. I stopped. Which way? Everything looked alike. Had I been crazy to come so far from the island? For Jane's sake, I kept my spirits up. If we couldn't rest here...

Then I saw a huge, familiar boulder with a white star.

"Right turn," I said, breathing out a happy sigh. "Your dad used to climb up on that boulder. He played King of the Castle." I wondered where my own cruel king was at the moment. Pounding his desk now that he had lost our signal? Hiring an investigator like Del? He would know that I had found help. But I hadn't told Del our plans.

We drove on another few kilometers. A weathered plank on a tree caught my eye. *Sinclair*, it read. *Three miles*. The days before metric.

"Is that it, Mom?" Jane asked at the end of a long and hilly road. She'd heard Andy talk about the place. His first .22. Hunting for deer and partridges. Then getting a bigger gun for moose and bear. "It's so tiny. Like in a fairy tale."

I got out and watched my breath steam in the cool air. The cabin was even smaller than I had remembered. A bit shabby, like a lost dog. The key to the padlock hung on a hook under the windowsill. Weeds and saplings crowded the clearing. The cedar-shingle roof had some moss, but seemed solid.

Andy's grandpa had built the place with a couple of hunting buddies and a chainsaw.

All of them must have passed by now. I suspected that someone from the reserve kept an eye on it for Andy. They might not know about his death.

Gramps had said that a good cabin would outlive us all.

The door creaked open. A musty smell met my nose. Everything looked exactly the same. About twenty by twenty with a sturdy Fisher woodstove. No cheap tin jobs for Gramps. A Canadian Tire wall calendar from a decade ago. The pump at the sink would work until the hard freeze. After that, we would get our water from the creek or later melt snow for drinking and bathing. It was nearly dark, but I felt relieved and safe. Joe would never find us. But could we make a life here?

"Let's start unpacking. Go get those lanterns. The kerosene cans are in the back of the Bronco. Welcome to the frontier,"

I said to Jane, rubbing her shoulders. She smiled back. My little girl was a trooper.

In minutes we had all the light we would need. Tacked to one wall was a fading color picture of Andy and me. I remembered when Gramps took it with our Polaroid. A lump in my throat brought back the moment.

"Wow, Mom. You look so young," Jane said when I pointed it out.

I had hoped for a supply of wood, but I had been fooling myself. In the ten years since Gramps passed, any wood left in the shack out back would be eaten away by dry rot. No electricity. No heat. Often I'd chuckled over a book about someone living in the bush but with a complete four-piece bathroom with hot water. City people take comforts for granted. Most of them have no idea what an outhouse is.

I was glad for the double bed. We curled up together in our sleeping bags, hoping that our body warmth would cancel out the cold of the mattress.

The next day I drove into Fort Fraser. I found a notice advertising seasoned firewood at the Petro-Canada station and store. Using their phone, I ordered three cords.

The woodman chugged into our drive in a huge dump truck. Six hundred bucks. The wood looked clean. It was good value.

"Drop it over here, please. And you said you could pile it?"

"Sure can. Fifty dollars should do it. You best stand back," he said, picking up a wicked-looking hook and spearing the first chunk. He moved into a regular rhythm and the task was underway. Wood was cheaper here where it could be gleaned from the clear-cut timber lots after the logging.

Two hours later I put the cash into his hand. Sitting in a tarped pile by the house was a warm winter.

"You're lucky, ma'am. This was the last load I had. Don't wait so long next year." He tipped his wool hat complete with earflaps.

"I won't. Thanks." I added a tip. No tax in the underground economy.

"There's extra pine for the kindling," he said with a smile. "And a chopping block too. No charge. The birch will burn all night, not like the fir down south. Lots of coals in the morning."

He tooted his horn and waved as he left. His friendliness warmed my heart. In the North, people went out of their way to be kind. When the climate could kill, you stuck together. Those stranded could even break into a camp. Bush code. Isolation made me feel safe. No land line, no cell phone. No cable. No TV. At the cost of our lives, we wouldn't miss them.

Cooking was simple and fun. Creativity carried us. Stews, soups, beans and skillet bread. The old one-pot meals seemed best. People up here weren't used to fresh vegetables. When the temperature dipped below zero, we'd have all the freezer space we'd need in a shed. Pasta, rice and potatoes were our mainstays. The bears were long gone to their dens, and coons and foxes couldn't penetrate the locked door. Jane had told the spider in the outhouse to leave us alone for the winter. "Estivation," she called it. A kind of hibernation. Like we were doing.

# CHAPTER EIGHT

Our first week was the roughest. Chores kept us hopping. Even split and piled, wood warms you three more ways: hauling, burning and cleaning up the ashes. The snows were beginning, and the creeks froze over. I had never imagined how long it took to melt enough snow for a pan bath. No wonder the Scandinavians loved their saunas.

One morning, I opened the door of a small outbuilding and nearly started laughing. Tarped inside was the old Bombardier Ski-Doo snowmobile that

Andy and I had used on our honeymoon. A tiny 250cc model—a baby next to today's muscular 1000cc versions. A set of tools sat on the spider-webbed wooden counter along with two empty gas cans. Everything was filthy with dust.

Jane clapped her hands. "A snow-mobile. I sure miss our rides from when I was a little kid. Do you think it still works? That would really be fun."

Grinning, I opened the cowling. "These things run forever. I bet I can get it going." I had done my share of the tune-ups on the older models at our shop. No fancy circuitry. Just the basics. Andy had said that I had the touch of an angel with a carburator.

A week later, a battered Jeep bumped down the drive. A man in a handsome beaded buckskin jacket got out. His raven hair swept over his brow. His arms were folded and his dark eyes flashed disapproval. This looked like trouble.

I left the porch, where I'd been hammering a loose board. It couldn't be someone Joe sent. Not this soon. I forced a smile. Friend or enemy?

"This is reserve land," he said. "I'm presuming you didn't break into the cabin to survive." He tossed a look at our car.

I extended my hand. Jane came around the corner with an armful of wood. The happy look on her face vanished as she stopped in her tracks: were we safe or not?

"I'm Sandra Sinclair. Andy was my husband." I struggled to remember the few words Gramps had taught me. "Hadih." *Hello.*

"I'm Pat Redwing. Daint'oh." *How are you?* The tension in his voice eased.

"Soo'…" I shook my head. "It's been a long time. I never was much good at other languages. Flunked French."

"Soo'ushah is the reply. I am impressed." Looking around, he said, "So where is the guy? It's been years. And is this your little one? I have a daughter in high school."

"Andy passed a few years ago."

Pat lowered his head. "I didn't know that. Sorry for your loss. We were kids together."

"Come on in for a coffee, Pat," I said.

With our boots at the door, in snowy-country tradition, we sat at the table. Jane curled up with a book of animal tracks. She had spotted a lynx print near the lake.

As we sipped at the kitchen table, he asked, "So you were here about fifteen years ago? Nothing's changed, as you can see."

"I didn't know what to expect. I mean, Tom died not that long after Jane was born. We were so busy with the shop that the time got away from us, I guess. That's why we never managed to come back here."

"I miss old Tom. We pass by the camp every now and then to see that it's okay. In case Andy came up." He drained the cup and gave me a nod of thanks. "But surely you're just visiting. Can't be that you want to spend the winter. You know how brutal it gets."

"Pat, I'm going to trust you with some information. I'd rather that no one knew I was here for now. At least not under my real name."

He gave me a curious look but said nothing.

I brushed back my hair in a nervous gesture. "There's a very dangerous man looking for us. He has powerful connections."

Pat put his hand on his heart. "I'm sorry for your troubles. No one will bother you. You have my word on that. Tom's family is part of my own blood. Do you have everything you need? You're gonna have to rough it big-time."

I laughed. "You forget that I lived in Dawson Creek. That's a climate and a half."

He leaned forward over the table. "Fishing's good. Lots of trout. In the winter we take our ice huts out too."

"I'm thinking of getting the old snowmobile going again. Could you keep your eye out for a used blower for the drive? For a while I can crunch the snow down, but I'll be bogging soon enough even with four-wheel drive."

When he left, I realized that I had a friend. It was as if I had found a new planet. Joe seemed so far behind. By now he would have thrown out a dragnet in every direction. I prayed that our tracks to the North had been covered.

Not for the first time, I wished that I could have brought Bonnie with me. But in her confused state, how could I? She was safe where she was.

Would we ever see her again?

\* \* \*

As the winter set in, I made sure that we had shovels and snow scoops. Pat arranged for a used snowblower in running order. It would make a path to the main road. That would be plowed before dawn each morning for the school buses. More than once he brought us a grouse for a special treat.

I thought about a weapon. Pistols were out. While I knew how to handle a shotgun and a .22 rifle, how could I carry one? Getting a gun license might be tricky too. I'd have to take a handling course. Not good for a low profile.

Jane, aka Denise, was now in school. The process was smooth. I stood tall and sounded confident when I enrolled her. Families relocated. Records were lost in fires. Every week we went into the little branch library to check out more books and use the Internet.

I cautioned Jane. "I know it's hard, but you're not to send any emails to your friends. You understand why."

"Duh, of course, Mom. I took my Facebook page down before we left. Twitter too. Is it always going to be this way?"

"Sweetie, I know this is hard. We talked about it before we left. You can make new friends as long as you don't use your real name." Her story was that we'd lived in Vancouver before I lost my job. I was now a writer working from home. Who wasn't writing a novel these days? Meanwhile, I had us signed up for health cards so that we would get medical care at the local clinic. God bless Canada.

The money was holding out well. We had no rent and no utility bills. Only our food, gas and occasional propane. The ax and hatchet took care of heating needs. Jane had put herself in charge of the wood. She had an eagle eye for splitting. Grandpa Tom's genes. Still, I prayed that she never had an accident. The North could be unforgiving. Not evil and indifferent. That was one difference between Joe and the mountain lion. The beast killed to survive, whereas the man killed for sport.

One day in early December, at the small supermarket, I picked up a copy of the *Vancouver Sun*. I felt like screaming for joy. Joe was under investigation. They weren't sure if it was going to go to trial. He had the best Toronto lawyer that money could buy. The man had gained notoriety for plea bargaining for the wife of a serial killer. Everyone knew that the woman was as guilty as her husband. Now she was free after having only served a few years.

As for Joe's case, the words *misunderstanding* and *exaggeration* suggested that dementia had played a role. He was blaming his victims. His estate had been built on lies and abuse of the vulnerable. Cleverly, he avoided the richest prey with interested heirs. Ten or twenty thousand at a time satisfied him.

I stuffed the paper into a trash can.

Now I could breathe for a while.

# CHAPTER NINE

When the serious snow arrived in January, I had the snowmobile all geared up. Twenty years old, but the engine ran like a Swiss watch.

First, an oil change. Then a new spark plug. The belt was threadbare, so I got a gently used one at the dealer in town. I also duct-taped the ripped leatherette seat. Bombardier had built Canada on these babies. If the car industry had been as efficient, no one would have needed a new model.

Under that clear blue sky that defines the wilderness, Jane and I explored our new home. The established trails were enough for us. Breaking our own might have bogged us in soft snow. We'd putt along on Holy Cross Lake, then follow the connection into a chain of smaller lakes. Fluffy coats began to cover the conifers. Rabbits' fur had turned to white. I wished for the same camouflage.

"Be careful around where creeks enter and where lakes join," I told Jane. "When the water is running underneath, the ice gets thin. You can't tell until it's too late."

"That's what Dad always told me," she said. "You don't know what's below the surface."

We had bought used snowmobile suits with flotation and helmets. Every year in BC a dozen people drowned riding snowmobiles. Sometimes they crashed. More often they went down riding too soon or too late on the lakes. Men, for the most part. It was in their nature to take risks.

Sometimes we stopped for lunch and ate sandwiches and dried fruit. I'd make a small fire from spruce twigs and we'd boil water in a tiny billy can for tea or hot chocolate. Nothing tasted as good as a hot drink outdoors. When the temperature sank to forty below, it kept us inside a few days at a time. Too cold for even the school bus. But those low temperatures also meant we didn't get the 10 meters of snow like Revelstoke down south. Fine with me.

"Do you think we're safe?" Jane would ask at the dinner table.

"Safe as we can be, honey," I'd answer. After a while, she seemed to relax in her new life.

But I'd seen that look in Joe's eyes. There was a reason Scout had been dumped. Joe had made a mistake when he thought an active young border collie would stay alone without barking. Admitting that he had been wrong was impossible.

When Joe invested, he got his money's worth...or else. I tried not to imagine the fury when he found us gone. The cold resolve as the weeks and months passed. The idea paralyzed me. We had to be sharp and alert.

With more free time, I caught up on the island news at the library's computer link. I noted an obituary for Bonnie. We should have been there to say goodbye. Taking a chance, from a pay phone I called her next-door neighbor, Sharon.

"Sandra, my god, where have you been?"

"I can't explain. It's been impossible to call. What happened to Bonnie? I just read—"

"She's gone to glory, honey. It happened so suddenly. One morning I went over and she was cold in bed. They think her heart just stopped. Or a stroke. She didn't suffer. What a mercy."

"If I could have been there..." A sob died in my throat. The times we'd talked in her cozy cottage returned to me. Bonnie laughing and teasing. Her common sense about raising Jane. Her warm embrace with a little squeeze at the end. I knew that she wished us well and happy. That was all that counted now.

"Bonnie loved you. She's in a better place now and understands. Like we all will someday." Sharon told me that everything was under control.

"I can't thank you enough." The woman had taken care of the simple cremation and cleaned out the rented house. The ten thousand dollars left belonged to her. She'd earned it.

"Bonnie and I were…close. It was hard to see her fail so quickly. But it happens. Her sense of time was a problem. A day, a week, a month. She lived in the moment."

"Did you see Joe visit her?" I asked. Bonnie would have mentioned him.

"You mean that fellow in the fancy suv? It's odd, but he was there last week, the day before she passed. She could still take care of herself, but she was losing it upstairs. She told me how he had brought her a lovely fruit basket and a box of chocolates."

"What else did she say about me?" I held my breath until my lungs hurt. Joe visiting her could mean big trouble.

"She said that she missed you and hoped you'd come back soon. That last night when I went in to see how she was before bed, she was muttering about some cabin. Bonnie was pretty confused by that time."

An icicle of fear in my rib cage chilled me more than the worst blizzard. Talking about a cabin. Somehow Bonnie had remembered Gramps and his hunting from when she had been a child.

It was time to go. If I planned it right, we could leave in a week. Maybe three days.

How long would it take for him to locate the camp and get up here?

With all the resources in the world? Was I kidding myself?

He might already be on his way.

I stopped blowing the drive after that. We rode in and out from the main road on the snowmobile. The harder the access for him, the better.

# CHAPTER TEN

The next day was Friday, the Ides of March. Jane had been reading *Julius Caesar* for her English lesson. The Roman general had gone to the forum against all advice and taken umpteen stab wounds.

I felt the same pain when I saw Joe's 1-LGL-EGL suv parked in front of the Yamaha shop as I walked by. Their sign said: *Snowmobile Sales and Rentals*.

I forced myself to calm down by taking deep breaths. My heart was rattling in my chest. Time slowed to a trickle.

An old lady on a walker crossed the street. I heard each crunch of the frame. Lift, down, lift, down.

My stomach twisted.

I didn't see Joe. The rentals were kept behind the store. With shaking hands, I put up my parka hood and walked to the car.

He didn't know my Bronco, but so what? In this tiny town, newcomers stuck out, especially women alone. How could I have told everyone to watch out for him? I had some pride, stupid though that sounded. If he asked enough people…

It had barely been a week since Bonnie died. Joe had moved quickly. He once had told me that he'd driven for thirty-six hours to Mexico to reach a client when planes were grounded. Taking amphetamines, of course. I ducked and eased into the Bronco, pulling away slowly. The last thing I needed was to attract attention.

I picked Jane up at school instead of letting the bus bring her home. "Joe's here," I said as she loaded her books into the car.

I might as well have slapped her across the face. No panic, though. My daughter had been rock solid from the time she'd learned to walk and talk. Jane allowed herself a deep breath, then straightened up like a soldier. "What are we going to do, Mom?"

She had brought her gear to town for a sleepover with a girlfriend. I thanked all the gods for the miraculous timing. "I'll take you to Karen's. Stay there until you hear from me. That should be Saturday morning."

"But...if I don't..."

"You will, baby."

"He won't leave us alone, will he?" For the first time, she looked at me woman to woman. It was my fault that she was growing up far too fast.

"No. You are absolutely right." I wouldn't lie to her when our lives were in jeopardy.

"What are you going to do? Can you get a gun?" Her small jaw clenched in worry. "What about taking off tonight? I could be packed in half an hour. Even less. We don't need much."

A thousand escapes. A thousand new towns. Who could live like that?

"It's way too late. You're not to worry about me. If it's one thing I know, it's the bush. Your dad taught me well."

When I dropped her off, I hugged her like there was no tomorrow. Part of me was rational, and part was running on adrenaline. What would happen to her in the worst scenario? I shut my mind to any possibility other than success. That was what Joe would have done.

Joe had enough money to buy help, maybe from out of town. But I knew he would come alone. His pride ruled him. That's why he drove the suv, like a signature stallion in battle. I counted on that assumption.

I hoped it would not be my last mistake.

I was the bait, not the prey. For once he wouldn't be in control, even if he thought he was. He'd lived his life counting on the trust and innocence of others, like his first wife. Forewarned is forearmed, my grandpa once said.

The weather was my friend. It had been unusually warm for March. Temperatures had nudged above freezing. Snowmelt from the mountains swelled the streams. The lakes were on the verge of channeling at the edges before break up. But the ice was still almost a meter thick in places. Sometimes daredevils snowmobiled until the end of April. Not this year. Everyone jokes about snowmobile soup, but it's a sad fact of northern life. Usually alcohol is a factor. And speed.

I'll say one thing for Joe. He had taught me to plan.

We had our flotation suits. And I'd added a pair of emergency ice picks, to be worn on a leather thong around the neck. Without them, you couldn't climb back on the ice. It would keep breaking until you lost consciousness from hypothermia. Five dollars saved your life. Ounces of prevention. Those who called them "sissy" were fools. When seconds counted, precision was important. I thought about Jack London's story "To Build a Fire." Stranded in the bush, a man used his last match to light a life-saving blaze.

He didn't count on the snow falling from a branch far above.

Flame out. Game over.

This was not going to happen to me.

Sounds funny, but a fast sled can travel over water as long as it keeps going at top speed. That was the irony. My safe old machine went far too slow. I was counting on that. And on Joe's triumph in catching me.

I almost laughed when I remembered what Bonnie had said. "You chase after a man until he catches you."

Had she really died in her sleep? Without suspicious circumstances, there had been no autopsy. Her heart had stopped.

Stopped? I wondered now. Or been stopped?

No time to think about it.

Holy Cross Lake was about 32 kilometers by 16. The last ice hut had been hauled off two days ago. Only the tracks of the sled skis remained.

My vehicle was waiting at the head of our road. I left a few things on display. A familiar sweater, scarf, paperback mystery. For sweetening, I could imagine the feral growl he would give upon seeing them. Then he'd notice that there was no way to drive in the final 5 kilometers.

At the dealership he would rent the best and largest. No one needed lessons on those machines. Pull off the kill switch. Push-button start. Snowmobiles had no gearshifts, regardless of their size and speed. Brake handle on one side, a strong thumb on the other.

But he was no bushman. Over-confidence and unfamiliarity with the rules would be his weaknesses. So I hoped.

I undid my faithful Ski-Doo from the tree I'd chained it to and chugged my way to the cabin. Hill after hill. Untouched fresh snow showed that he hadn't come yet. Some innocent person at the post office or library would have helped this smiling man. They'd tell him where I lived. A woman alone and a young girl. Arrived not long ago. How many of us could there be? Would he be carrying a wrapped present, a "surprise" for my birthday? He was good at surprises. But so was I.

I parked the sled behind of the house, checked the oil and gassed up. Then I went inside and grabbed something to eat. A can of tuna, a chocolate bar. My stomach was knotted and protesting, but I shoveled in the fuel anyway and gulped hot tea.

I checked my watch. Six and dark already. When the clouds scudded aside, the full moon illuminated the paper birches. The lofty spruce and pine stood sentinel.

I knew exactly where to take him. The weak spot on the lake where the creek comes in. It had been gurgling since the beginning of the melt. Fresh snow dustings made it look pristine. All I had to do was get him to follow me. Instead of fleeing, I was leading him to his death.

I waited a long time. Jane would be in bed at her friend's by now. They'd planned to watch scary movies after dinner. The trust Jane had placed in me kept me from screaming my rage to the heavens. I blamed myself for sending us into the clutches of this calculating monster. What good was guilt now? Action was the only answer. I thought of the happiest moments in my life. Saying "I do" to Andy. Holding Jane in my arms for her first meal, a tiny bubble on her rosebud lips. Watching with glowing pride every step that she took.

At last it turned midnight. Joe knew I never stayed up after eleven. The quilted suit was bulky. My feet were going to sleep in the heavy boots. Sweat had soaked the long underwear beneath. I took another drink of cold tea. Then my ears twitched like a rabbit's.

A big machine charged along the main road. Its huge bright eye filtered through the trees. Slipping out through a back window, I crept to my Ski-Doo.

Joe pulled up in front of the house and left his engine running. *Brrrrap. Brrrrap.* Making a loud and aggressive entrance pleased him.

Inside the house, two lanterns burned. It was obvious that I had no electricity, no landline nor cell coverage. To him, I was alone and helpless.

A leg cramp from tension dropped me to my knees. I bit my lip and tasted the coppery blood as he clomped up the front steps. Would this be like a nightmare where I would try to run but find my body paralyzed?

"Sandra!" he called. "I know you're in there. All I want to do is talk to you. Be reasonable. I've come a long way."

I clapped my hand over my mouth to keep from laughing. Reasonable was the last thing he was. I'd learned that on the wrong end of his anger.

He pounded on the locked door. *Bam! Bam!* Then he kicked at it. I didn't care. It would put him into exactly the right mood for his adventure. I hoped Jane wouldn't panic and make them bring her back tonight. That's a large load to leave on a child, but this wasn't a perfect world.

"And you pawned Granny's ring," he said. "That hurt. But I'm a big man, Sandra. I can forgive you. We can make a fresh start."

I said nothing, just braced myself and gripped the pull handle, counting down. Timing was everything.

"Jane? Where's my little girl? I have a present for you." All was silent except for the pulse of blood in my ears. From far away, I heard a wolf howl. Then the door burst open. Glass shattered. My heart was in my throat.

Thumps and crashes sounded as he moved like a bull through the house. Everything smashed in his wake. He would have been pleased to think that we were hiding, shaking, anticipating his justice.

A howl of anger rose from inside the cabin.

Why had I waited so long? I pulled the throttle.

Nothing but resistance. One tug usually did it.

A hot fist clutched at my chest. I hadn't counted on this. "Come on, baby. Do it for Mother," I said. I closed my eyes. Pulled again.

And she kicked in.

Snow flew in my wake as I rocketed down the trail. I knew every last meter. He'd follow my fresh tracks on the packed snow. I'd thought about stringing a thin wire across the trail to behead him. As fast as he'd be going, he wouldn't see it. But putting it up beforehand might have injured someone else.

"*Who cooks for you?*" asked the barred owl from its perch high above. The owls were safe in their nests, raising their chicks. Would I ever find sanctuary for mine?

We took the circular trail around the lake. Up and down, around corners. He couldn't gain on me with those twists and turns. And yet at the ice, I wanted him closer. About 6 meters behind. I had thought about it a thousand times, playing and replaying the tape in my head.

Finally I hit the approach to the lake. It plummeted down a steep hill. And 30 meters out was the bull's-eye I wanted to strike. From a distance, the surface looked fine and glassy. Some ice was six inches and some was half an inch. Eroded from currents fanning out below. Hard to tell unless you were standing near it.

As he closed in to 15 meters, I gunned the machine and swept down onto the lake. I could hear him raging. He knew that he could catch me. I threw off my helmet and it bounced behind, cannonballing off his windshield.

He roared in triumph, as if I had tossed it from desperation. The rush he was feeling would outweigh common sense. Despite his intelligence, he was operating on adrenaline alone. Or perhaps those pills. On the level of a wild beast.

Just as he closed in on the straightaway, the ice broke. I went into the water, the machine sinking below me as I kicked free and swam for my life. It wasn't as bad as I'd thought. The suit protected my core. For a moment my lungs threatened to seize. Four meters deep on the maps. Two would be more than enough. As long as he was in over his head.

Buoyant, my face and ears stinging with cold, I clambered to the edge of the jagged hole. With the helmet gone, I wasn't disoriented. In the panic, he might not get his off at all. I was counting on that. Straps and snaps were impossible to work with heavy mitts or frozen hands.

Following so closely, he wouldn't be able to stop. An experienced rider might have gunned the machine over the water like Jesus walking. Joe panicked and braked. The machine flipped 180 degrees as it slid toward 10 meters of open water. The heavy back end went in first, trapping him beneath.

The windshield closed over his head as the machine dropped like a stone. It must have been like wrestling a refrigerator.

Somehow he bobbed to the top. Joe was strong.

As he thrashed, I pulled the picks from around my neck and hauled myself out with a groan. All the activity at the cabin had made me strong. I wasn't the same grieving woman he'd met at the bluffs, slipping into a patch of nettle. Happy to be helped to her feet.

One hand, another, left, right. Precious inch after inch to where the surface held. On my knees, then crawling.

At last I struggled upright and staggered 12 meters to a safe section. A rush of energy gave me the surge I needed as I looked back at the man who had put me and my daughter through hell. My feet were icy blocks, but I kept walking. Call it the life force. Or maybe Andy's smile was pushing me forward.

Joe's gloved hand flipped up his visor as he splashed.

"Help me! For god's s-sake, S-sandra." City people never think about flotation suits. Or ice picks. Knowledge is power. Especially in a killer environment. He was wearing a monster down coat that had become an icy coffin. His boots were probably filled with water.

"*God* has not said a word, Joe. Don't you find that interesting?"

At -15°C, it wouldn't take long for the ice to refreeze.

In the moonlight, I walked to the edge of the lake until I couldn't see him. Or hear his weakening screams. My teeth were chattering, but I was moving.

I started up the snowmobile trail and noticed a set of rabbit tracks. The moon had never been so bright. A white arctic hare hopped past me to the shelter of a cedar. We'd both survived tonight.

I retrieved a set of warm clothes and boots from the bush where I had left them in a garbage bag. I broke open several sets of hand warmers for my hands, feet, neck and groin.

No one would blame me for saving myself. They would take it on faith that I made it to the cabin despite being soaked. Northerners did that. They had to.

In ten minutes Joe would be dead from hypothermia. My one sorrow was that he wouldn't suffer. His systems would shut down quickly and painlessly. I thought of his first wife.

This was sweet revenge for Chrissie.

I started humming "Home Sweet Home" as I began my trek. Joe, Joe, you taught me so much. But where was *your* contingency plan?

2190 miles, Apelachian

2650